George and the New Craze

By Alice Hemming

Illustrated by Kimberley Scott

There was a new craze at the Heavenly Hippos Wildlife Park. People Cards!

The penguins had the full collection
– all one hundred People Cards.

George had three cards. He was very pleased with them, even though two were the same.

He kept them safely on his fence. He couldn't decide which order was best.

Every so often, he shuffled them around.

Seymour had one card. It was a rare one.
"What do we do with People Cards?" he asked.
George wasn't sure.

They tried to build a tower but there weren't enough cards.

'Snap!' didn't work with just one pair.

And when they put them in an album
there were too many gaps.

"Let's look for some cards," said George.
Seymour wasn't sure.
"Mine looks lovely all by itself," he said.
"It's a rare one."

"OK," said George, "but I'm going to look for some more."

George found one. It was fine
once he'd cleaned it up a bit.

George bumped into Toni.
"What are you doing?" he asked.

"Looking for People Cards," said Toni.
"I would love to have the full collection."
"Me too," said George. "Hey – why don't
we share our cards?"

Toni thought that was a great idea.

So did Gus.

And Mo and Max.

And even Minnie.

All together, they had ninety-nine different
People Cards and lots of spares!

They could do all sorts of things with ninety-nine People Cards.

They built the tallest tower at the Heavenly Hippos Wildlife Park.

And they had some fun and fast-paced games of Snap!

But they still couldn't fill up the album.
"We just need one more card," said George.

"I think I have the one you need," said Seymour in a small voice.

Gilbert
Gilbert is a lorry driver. He also plays the drums in a band.

Alice
Alice is an author. She likes rainy days.

Filippo
Filippo is a librarian. He has travelled to hundreds of different countries.

Clara
Clara is a schoolgirl. Her favourite animal is a platypus.

Mara
Mara is a horse rider. She loves to ride and care for her horses.

The Queen
The Queen wears a shiny crown. She enjoys summer garden parties.

Sonia
Sonia is a hairdresser, and she loves to sing karaoke.

Rajit
Rajit is a veterinary surgeon. He bakes a lovely raspberry cheesecake.

Tommy
Tommy is a little boy. He rides his bike super-fast.

Babette
Babette is a security guard. Her favourite colour is green.

Steve
Steve is a publisher. He wears extremely colourful shirts.

Kimberley
Kimberley is an illustrator. She likes to do Yoga and stand on her head.

"It looks great!" said Seymour, when he saw his card with all the others.

"Let's show the penguins!" said George.

But the penguins weren't collecting People Cards any more. There was now a brand new craze at the Heavenly Hippos Wildlife Park!

The End

George's New Craze
is an original concept by
© Alice Hemming

Illustrator: Kimberley Scott
Represented by Advocate Art

ISBN 978-1-84886-204-3

A CIP catalogue record for this book is
available at the British Library.

Published by
MAVERICK ARTS PUBLISHING LTD

Studio 3A, City Business Centre, 6 Brighton Road,
Horsham, West Sussex, RH13 5BB

© Maverick Arts Publishing Limited May 2016
+44 (0)1403 256941

Sonia

Sonia is a hairdresser,
and she loves to sing
kara...

Maverick
arts publishing
www.maverickbooks.co.uk